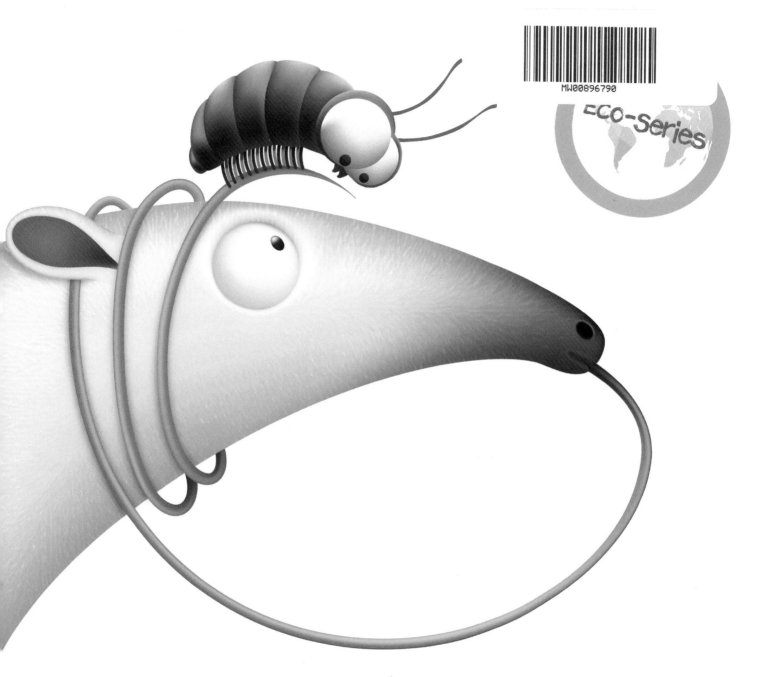

ECO-Series

Harrison
By: Michelle Tucker

To unique friendships everywhere

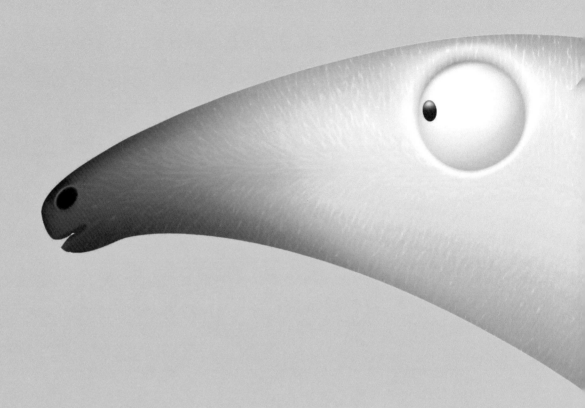

Harrison: A Star-Studded Friendship
Eco-Series Book 2
Copyright ©2015 by Michelle Tucker
All Rights Reserved
Published in the United States, Washington, DC
CIP data is available
ISBN: 978-0-9965267-3-9
[1. Friendship-Fiction. 2. Anteater-Fiction.
3. Insects-Fiction.]

Eco-Series

The Eco-Series books stem from a passion to foster an enhanced understanding of our amazing earth and it's Animal Kingdom.

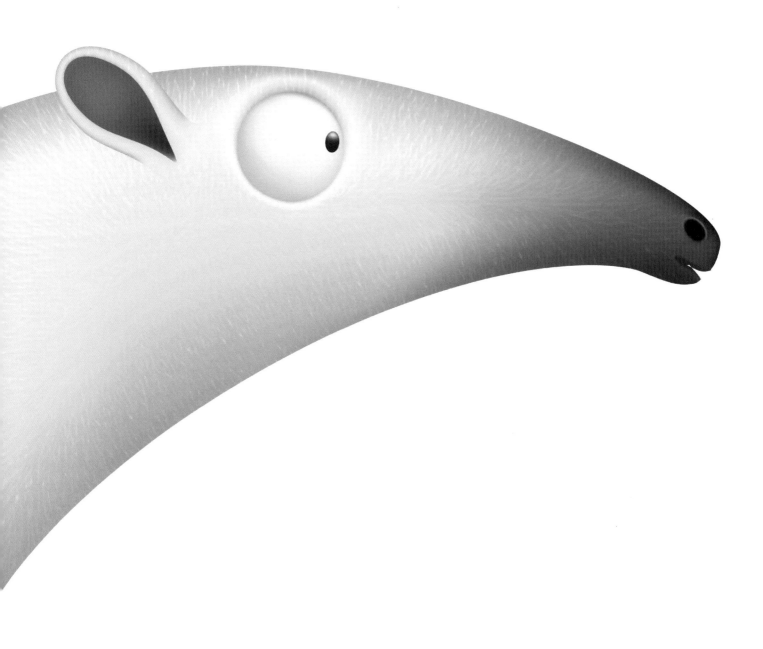

Harrison was a friendly Anteater.

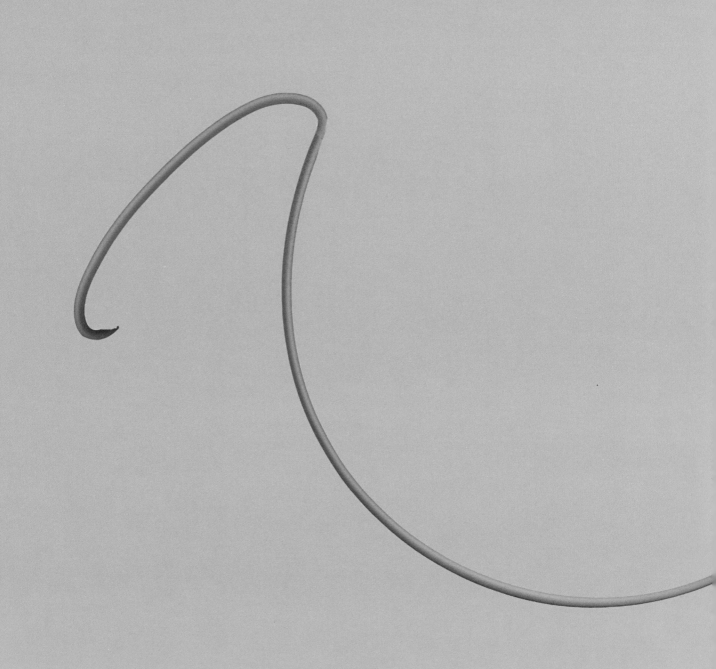

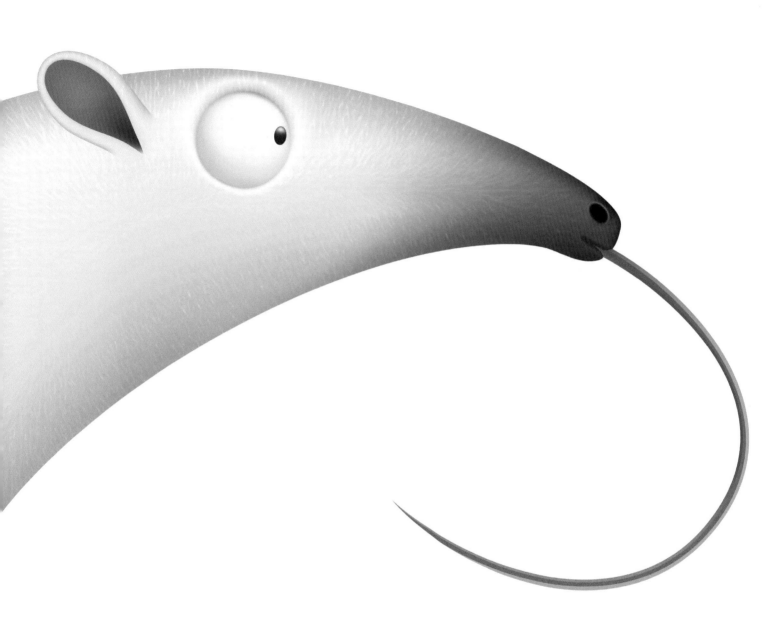

Although, when it was time to eat, he never ate ants!

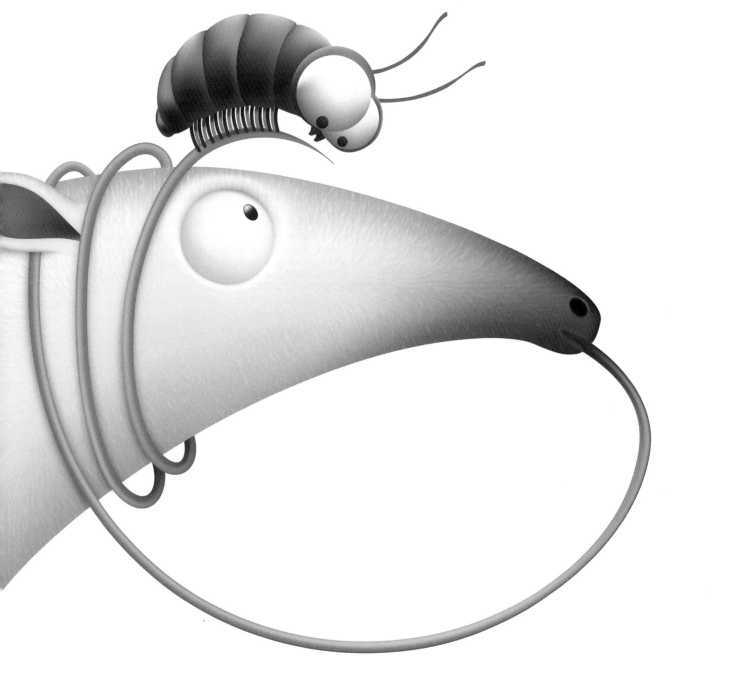

In fact, he loved ants! Especially his best friend Sofia. They spent their days together having fun.

When Harrison and Sofia first met, he sometimes worried that Sofia would be afraid of him.

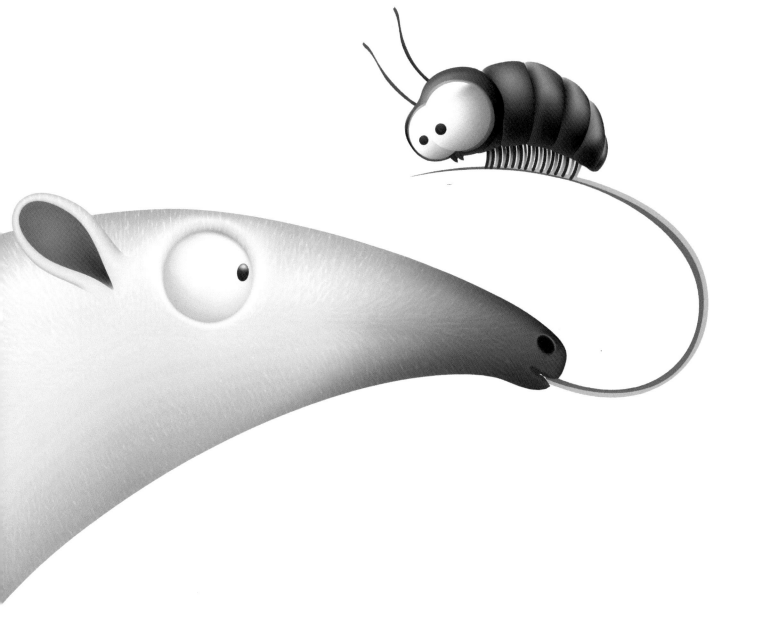

But she never seemed to be! Still, he worried that their friendship might not last.

So, Harrison was always thinking of new
ways to entertain Sofia.

often, he woud take Sofia out at night
and point out the stars and planets in
the big sky.

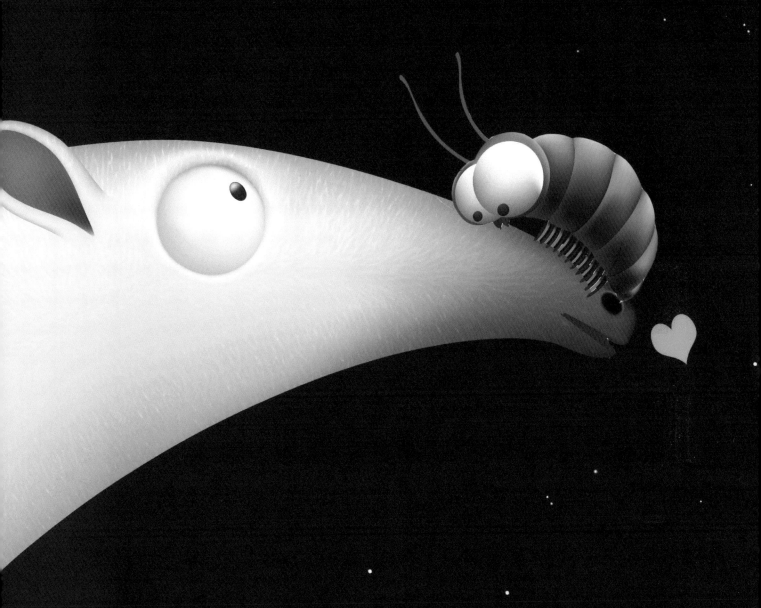

Sofia loved it so much she gave Harrison
a big kiss. And then he knew for sure
that their friendship would last.

Other Books By Michelle Tucker

Paleo Stomp!

Paleo Stomp!
By: Michelle Tucker

Dogs Can't Paint!

Dogs Can't Paint!
By: Michelle Tucker

Author Bio

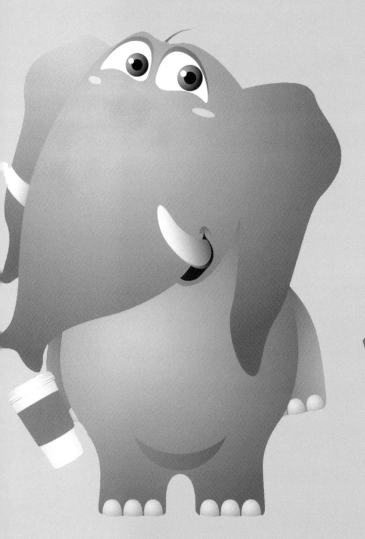

Michelle Tucker is an Author and Animal Lover, who can't cook, and drinks way too much coffee. She lives in the Washington DC area with her fantastic husband and kids, and their menagerie of silly pitbulls.

Visit Michelle online at:
http://www.mwbesuppliers.com

CPSIA information can be obtained at www.ICGtesting.com
Printed in the USA
LVIW01n1200120217
524028LV00002B/43